FABLE

Theodore Lownil
Illinois Benedictin
Lisle, Illinois

FABLE

Robert Pinget

Translated by Barbara Wright

Red Dust / New York / 1980

Originally published as *Fable*
by Les Editions de Minuit, Paris 1971
Copyright © Les Editions de Minuit 1971

This translation is published in Great Britain as *Fable*
by John Calder (Publishers) Ltd. London 1980
© This translation, Barbara Wright 1980

Published in the United States of America
by Red Dust, Inc., 1980

Library of Congress Catalogue Card Number: 80-50203
ISBN 87376-036-0

The publication of this book has been made possible in part by a grant from
the National Endowment for the Arts in Washington, D.C., a Federal Agency.

to
Alberto

Looking for somewhere to spend the night he stopped at an abandoned barn, went in, made a hole in the hay and fell asleep in it, his knapsack under his head.

But someone had seen him in the moonlight, a belated traveler.

There are times of initial despair which alternate with others when the soul is liberated but little by little the alternation stops and that's when the head begins to rot.

Did he think about it before he fell asleep or did he only count the beams in the roof.

And that other belated person.

The town had evaporated as a result of a cataclysm, nothing was left but the dross.

The people were camping in little groups in the ruins or making their way into the fields.

This future to be dissolved.

A man called Miaille or whatever but the time isn't ripe.

Poppies in the morning were reddening in the oats.

So the night is over.

He goes off to the blazing meadow and he says poppies for the children, fading nosegays, far away years, far away and pleasant.

He takes some cheese out of his knapsack and a bottle of wine.

7

FABLE

Naked men with leather belts come out of the river and make their way towards the corpse lying on the bank. They carve it up with the knives hanging from their belts and start to devour it. Their leader has reserved the phallus for himself and he makes short work of it before starting on the groin.

Or those clusters of delphiniums when June starts yellowing in the fields.

A little kitchen garden full of aromatic herbs.

It seems he didn't go straight to sleep, but counted the beams in the roof, attaching the day's images to them, the poppies, the naked men, the ruins of the town.

The corpse on the river bank was that of a boy with white skin and blue hair, as beautiful as ivory and ultramarine.

But the men attacked it again, carved it up again, devoured it all but its head which they hung from the leader's saddle. They went off at a gallop.

And he saw the people coming up behind and all the golden landscape, his beard was covered with poppies, his eyes were open.

It was the images of the night that made his head heavy now, all the pleasant years, far away and pleasant, like a ton of vomited sugar or a stinking defecation.

The past to be dissolved likewise.

Little by little the alternation stops.

Very little landscape, some yellow on the plain, a few trees, the time is still not ripe.

This present which made him speak, not to know any more what it's composed of.

I can see that rotting, bleeding head attached to the saddle.

And always the groups of exiles picnicking, tins of food, greasy papers, pallid faces, they go off then stop then go off again.

The town still smoking.

8

A house that was ours he said and here I am among the exiles eating dry bread and weeping endlessly from one stop to another, from one night to another, untl the day when this possession will be no more than a photo in my pocket between my passport and a postcard.

And no longer see.

And only just hear.

Just a muffled, inarticulate lament, perceive it piecemeal then lose it then pick up its harmonics again on the threadbare old string of the instrument eviscerated by the barbarians.

Lament, lament again, the poppies are fading and the photo is yellowing in his pocket, it was put there yesterday, centuries of avalanches, of clashes, of mortal wounds.

This Miaille[1] or whatever his name is who found himself alone in the barn which he later recognized, he found his way back there by instinct, he weeps until morning and then until the following night, he can't bring himself to leave the place, an old conformist, time has done its work, made into the past what even yesterday was still the unique present.

He went the rounds of the barn again, and the stable and the farm buildings, still carrying his knapsack for fear that the other man, the moonlight observer, might come and take it from him.

It contains neither wine nor cheese but letters, letters, diary notes, laundry bills, eating-house bills, notes written in haste, goes the rounds of the farm buildings, pulls up a nettle here, replaces a stone there, mortal wound, the merciless sun dissolves all that remained of a tenderness in which no one recognizes himself any more.

A little kitchen garden full of aromatic herbs.

When June starts yellowing in the fields, the delphiniums, unless they are his tears, turn blue, the sky is reflected in them.

When June brought the table back under the arbor, the

9

midday and evening aperitif, old conformist, yesterday's old tenderness in which neither furtive kisses nor hours spent by the fireside recognize themselves any more.

And why is it that that town, those ruins, why is it that those exiles in the fields who speak another tongue, only perceive it piecemeal—never spoken that language—why is it that they come back like someone else's obsession, that of the man in the moonlight or of the person who is absent.

There were absences in my life which were a comfort he said, then there was a presence that ruined me.

Still going the rounds of the farm buildings, he pulls up a nettle here, replaces a stone there, when all of a sudden everything crumbles and the voice comes to him out of the ruins, he recognizes its timbre and its harmonics on that threadbare old string of the eviscerated instrument, he runs, it was a mirage, the sun was setting just as he was waking out of a nightmare, step by step going the rounds of the kitchen garden, the aromatic herbs of death, there is no possible time any more.

A blue cluster in which the phallus flowered, a white and pink rod, balls the color of virginia tobacco.

One single mouthful the leader made of it before starting on the groin where the flesh is so tender, blood was dripping down his hairy chest and down his stomach.

These sorts of public images.

To get a taste of other secrets as bitter as gall in the shadow of the years to be dissolved, this death accompanied by the aromatic herbs of the little garden overrun and invaded by the image and then by its own shadow and then by the never-ending darkness, the delphiniums and the corpse merge into a single faded sheaf that you can only just make out in the moonlight.

Then he lay down in the grass, he tried to go to sleep but the oppressively hot sun made him get up again and sit down under the nearby elm tree, he could see two people dressed in white robes walking along the road, one had his arm round the other's shoulder, he believed he could hear them composing a difficult letter, first learning it by heart, the one correcting the other, the other inspiring the one, and with a common voice repeating the phrase dragged up out of the fathomless depths of their consciousnesses, they disappeared into the wood.

Where the only thing that might happen would be an attack by savages but an attack so thoroughly confused with the agonies of the nightmare that the recipient, the reader purified by the lost years, would grasp nothing of it but a vague grief transcribed in puerile terms, no symbols and even fewer reminiscences.

From his knapsack he once again extracts the so-called fatal letter and in rereading it discovers nothing but an adventure transcribed in the wretched, vulgar wording of a popular almanac, some charlatan must have dictated it, some rupture in time must have appropriated it and concealed it in the depths of its crevice like a secret that has no connection with the intangible peace that is his own and was such in his immemorial future.

Likewise to be dissolved.

To be dissolved and sown in the surrounding fields like the ashes of a Narcissus in one of those naive prints, a caricature for the use of concierges, those females who guard nothing but the imaginary.

The voice in the ruins, then, was double, dictating the letter that was in love with itself, reverberating over and beyond the herb garden on to the road like the steps of the people walking along it which simulate a language, such effrontery, but what's impossible about it in the circumstances in which only the person weeping in the grass turns over in his memory the poisoned phrase.

Two figures in white robes, their long hair plaited with oats and cornflowers, they went into the wood for their evening copulation, long ecstasy repeated until morning when their genitals separated in the dew.

FABLE

Come out of the wood as the sun is crossing the clearing and shake themselves in the poppies and then lick each other, their morning ablutions, then from the hollow of a tree pull out some honeycomb, their first meal.

But another atmosphere, that of a tormented conscience which only accepts controlled images, distorted in the direction of possible salvation, an old chimera when candor used to triumph on Easter mornings, the initiate finds himself back in the age of passions and lacking any sense of discrimination.

This obscure navigation between senses and reason which so far as we are concerned is no more than unadmitted duty, a rigidity that is even more unpracticed than it is sterile.

A blackbird whistled three notes.

There would be no more elm trees or farm buildings, there would be nothing but a room in the town smoking under its ruins, spared by a miracle in reverse, a deceptive refuge, a charnel house, death had been there from the first day and had gone unnoticed thanks to the neighboring premises not yet affected by the cataclysm, a sort of routine that aped life had become established.

It has to be accepted as it is, now, death in the midst of the ruins, going the fantastic rounds of a cemetery in which the only things that move are chimeras, the picnickers are sitting on the graves having their snacks before moving on to the next cemetery, that's the way they go about in the country that was once theirs, leaving behind them here and there those who can no longer follow, they get put under a slab with a flower in their hands, they've earned their rest.

The confused mass of possibilities before he yielded to what had to emerge, but what it was he didn't know, even though he had a presentiment of something serious he could no more than barely calculate its weight, tons of tears and vomit, maybe some connection with the destruction of the town and the hastily-erected cemeteries as if from the very

12

first day, that of its foundation, this city had not been menaced, madness to have built it within reach of the lava but the good weather had caused irresponsibility to triumph, years of sun and unruly and somewhat affected joy, they'd got the better of reason.

Looking for somewhere to spend the night he stopped at an abandoned barn, went in and suddenly in spite of the darkness recognized a certain layout, unchanged proportions which made him rediscover the echo of his steps on the mud floor then in the hay where he made a hole not to sleep in, sleep forsakes unhappiness, but to think about those lost years.

As for the belated traveler he was none other than that Miaille of bygone years, with blue eyes and blond beard, years of waiting, years of nothingness.

Watched himself stumbling in the darkness, soul adrift, hole in the hay like the lowest stable lad, he recognizes the echo of his footsteps on the mud floor.

As for the belated traveler he was none other than a foreigner, they'd commented on his accent at the bistro, from then on kept out of the way and prowled about at night in the moonlight.

That hope to be dissolved.

His eyes were still blue but his gaze was no longer the same, a sort of terror or vague humility, flight or renunciation, as for the emaciated face, the deteriorated dentition, the stooping carcass....

Time which is the petty, spasmodic malady, joy that forsakes, consciousness of all vanity, the carcass steers itself compassless toward its last resting place as if the theme of survival were henceforth obsolete.

Was thinking about that hodge-podge transformed by the magic of successive revelations, they were pretty precarious.

Unless they were only alive in so far as despair might have uprooted them.

13

FABLE

Suddenly as the memory of this thought comes back to him he sees the foreigner of former days looking at him, he wants to go up to him and give him his hand, but the other vanishes.

The sleep that has forsaken me is playing tricks on me, he says, but the other man's face was so innocent of all malice that he goes on looking for him in the dark and then gets up, goes out of the barn and walks over toward the road where earlier the white figures had been chatting.

But someone had seen him in the moonlight and was following him at a distance, not a ghost, a man of flesh and blood who is walking naked with a bunch of delphiniums in his hands, he can be seen approaching the kitchen garden where the aromatic herbs grow, he puts down his bunch of flowers and it comes back to life and stands up in the flower bed, it has never been picked, all its flowerets drinking the night air, the blue is very attenuated, attenuated.

Archangels' couplings. That sort of public image.

To taste other secrets as bitter as gall, so that it should no longer be a question of either beauty or of a comforter, will gradually resume the frightful solitude that breeds monsters and leads the dreamer to his destruction, that slab in the cemetery that he lifts up in order to slide underneath it and hear no more, is it true that death is deaf, that it's blind, that it no longer has the heart for the things that belong here below.

Unless they were only alive, these beliefs in survival, in so far as despair may have uprooted them, what fathomless depths to reach, no more question of the dreary frivolities of sex, no more question of revolt backed up with a plentiful supply of blasphemies, just the pure and simple horror of an attack of vertigo, one has to know.

A boy with white skin and blue hair, he had sat down on the bank, he was looking up at the sky, he stretched himself in the summer sun, he got up and ran into the splashing water, he laughed like a child, no one in this deserted place,

14

he swam a few breast strokes then came out still laughing, he lay down on the sand.

And the person observing him thinks this: that the victim is less to be pitied than the torturer.

That slab in the cemetery, maybe the observer is already underneath it, a little thought for him.

Or the Savior disfigured by torture, his face looms up on all sides in the mortal hours, or his circumcised sex organ.

There will be no necessity to separate what since childhood has been united, Sacred Heart and sacred ass, that hodge-podge in which no one recognizes himself until his last breath but it would be useless to add any further comment.

That shadow keeping watch on him, disappearing and then reappearing in the darkness or is it already daybreak, a bird was trying out a tune, the frogs had stopped croaking, a sort of calm reigned all around, not a breath, preceding the dawn, what has it in store for us, the drama to brood over all the day that is about to follow or a respite, a truce, the sleep, finally, that a sick, exhausted conscience doubts whether it deserves.

The town smoking under its ruins.

The boy with the delphiniums.

A shattered, rampant passion that adopts a multiple form to retrieve its scattered fragments, Proteus of despair.

Or from the opposite point of view a legend full of sentimental allegories, images profoundly rooted in the night of the soul which were seeing the light in this childish, picturesque and saccharin form but which none the less remained mortal for anyone who might take it upon himself to reverse its meaning, mortal since nothing that has anything to do with life, a word that has no meaning, remains innocuous for longer than a day, the time for a sunrise and a sunset, even time for love.

Or the sleep that forsakes unhappiness.

But an angel comes and tells him fear no more,

wherever you are, there I shall be whatever happens, or let us rather say that I have become your dream, no part of it from now on will ever be irretrievably lost, but alive and as necessary as any tiny little mechanical part is to a meticulous watchmaker, these will be the images that will animate your thoughts, whatever happens, whatever it costs me.

Now the angel was naked and crowned with poppies.

Then a second then a third joined him and together they performed the gestures of love and went into raptures in the morning grass.

A house that was ours he said and here I am among the exiles eating dry bread and weeping endlessly from one stop to another, but the angel said what do you know about destiny, a word that has no meaning, your dwelling-place is still the same, occupied by a breath that is also still the same, unchanged in spite of appearances, and do you know any more about appearances, perhaps yourself reflected in the eyes of anyone who looks at you, perhaps yourself.

There were absences in my life which were a comfort, then there was a presence that ruined me.

Endless sadness of all this tedious repetition, I want a new fable he said which would muster my energies for the last time, it would be the best of me but he went on lying in the hay, he heard the angel guffaw and the blackbird whistled Rise, take up thy bed.

He must have got up, then, gone the rounds of the farm buildings once again, the new fable would only emerge from ruins and deserted places, there would be no tedious repetition but rather a fervent will to say everything anew in order to renew everything.

Prolegomena.

A man called Miaille a stranger to the parts he lived in was one evening approached by a traveler who plants himself in the doorway and says let me unpack my suitcase here, I have chosen your dwelling-place, I'll be the maid and the gardener and the caretaker, I have finally come to the end of my afflictions, I saw this house from afar and hastened to it to find you, don't despise my services, I shall have others for your pleasure. The sedentary man opens his eyes wide and lets the traveler in.

Lived thus in oblivion, their gazes penetrating each other all day long, their thoughts the mirror one of the other, peace disseminated from the landscape over their minds and in their bodies, from their breaths over the landscape, an uninterrupted embrace prolonged even into their dreams, you had to call that happiness, now what is a gaze that penetrates another, what is a mirror, what is a dream, but the question was only asked after the mystery had been solved.

The one was reluctant to see it solved as anyone might be reluctant to cut a flower or to squash an insect, the other didn't give it any thought.

He was reluctant he said to see it solved, it was better to go no further than the premises but how to make them last *ad vitam*, the conclusion imposes itself with the force of a battering ram or of a shoot propelling itself out of a seed.

He heard the angel guffaw.

Their gazes not penetrating each other.

It's funny said the traveler, your eyes are like needles trying to pierce mine, you frighten me. And the sedentary man encouraged by this remark resorted to what he believed to be his power. Now that of the traveler did not reside in his eyes, they were only blank windows.

To say everything anew in order to renew everything.

But the angel disappeared leaving the dreamer in the hay, why get up it's barely dawn, this malady killing him won't go away by magic.

It was at the midday hour that he retraced the erstwhile path, going through the wood in which the white figures were loving each other, then through the fields along the road where the naked men were riding, with that blood-covered head attached to the saddle. To go beyond grief. A day will come when the new fable will emerge.

FABLE

To go beyond grief.

From that room like a watchtower.

That photo in my pocket he said between the passport and the postcard, the knapsack under my head full of sighing words. Nothing. There has never yet been any night that could put the head back on the truncated neck.

Or the business of the contents of the knapsack, bills from eating-houses or whatever which just as fast as they were compiled would reveal that vanished happiness.

Whiff of some old filth.

Reticule of a dead woman.

They find her lying on her kitchen floor with the gas pipe in her mouth, they all knew her in the neighborhood, a madwoman who passed herself off as a poetess, she knew a lot about that Miaille or whatever his name was, she'd frequented him all her life.

Modestly collect old straws in the wind.

Crossroads of possible directions.

The madwoman's reticule.

He remembered having seen her go by along the road holding her handbag against her stomach like a muff, dressed in woollies in the middle of the summer, red and sweating, telling her chaplet of doggerel the way a she-goat strings out her droppings, she went and sat down at the edge of the wood and took out of her reticule a diary in which she scribbled her poem, an old barcarolle, an old elegy which was unravelling itself in her brain and which she was trying to remember, suddenly gripped by enthusiasm and then sinking back into melancholy, then going into gales of laughter which made her stand up, walk round a tree then sit down again with a sob that dissolved into hiccups, doggerel, hiccups, she stood up again only in order to sit down again, started scribbling again, hiccuped once more, a quivering pythoness, a priestess of the pauperism into which her lonely, distorted soul had sunk.

18

He remembered having seen her in the company of white figures in the moonlight, lifting up her skirt and showing her behind to the devil whom she smelt out in the ditch or behind a little wall, exorcism, all three of them went into the wood, they could hear other people whispering and the old woman sat down on a tree trunk and watched the frolics and couplings as if she were at a strange Mass, here and there accepting in her mouth whichever stiff member approached her, they could hear her choking and spluttering, the vicious depraved old harpy, she kept on versifying, mixing the names of Christ and Mary with her obscene remarks to the hilarity of her companions.

He remembered having seen her riding pillion behind one of the horde of horsemen, she was tickling the bloodstained head dangling from the man's belt, she herself was shaking all over with her madwoman's laugh, the troop climbed hills and mountains and arrived at a corner of the firmament beyond the clouds where it scattered leaving the old woman between heaven and earth like a snowflake falling slowly, gently, down on to the grass where it melted at dawn, they found her shawl, her pince-nez that a lad went and returned to her in her kitchen, she's dozing in a chair, she starts, mumbles and versifies more than ever, producing a nursery rhyme that the child brings back either home or to school in mint condition.

These sorts of abandon.

Or the boy with the white skin who joined the others in the thicket and took part in their frolics.

These sorts of public images.

To taste other such secrets.

The alternation must take place, don't doubt it any longer, certainly redemptive, or rather giving way to a palpable serenity, installed in what should no longer be called either the heart or the brain but the soul perhaps representing the framework of all this disintegrating hodge-podge, the certainty of remaining alive, compact and without fissure *in aeternum*.

This present that makes him talk, not to know any more what it is composed of.

I can still see him bending over his notebook scribbling the poem he was trying so hard to remember, saying it over and over during his walk only to forget it again that evening, he takes up his pencil once more, scribbles again and versifies late into the night, the angel took possession of his sleep which he strewed with gulfs and mountains, intolerable awakening, had he slept, he was brooding over the old, long-vanished sadness, obsessed by time seen as a sequence of days, a precarious vision, everything must finally give way to....

I have chosen your dwelling-place.

It was one morning, the man called Miaille was barely emerging from sleep, was looking out of the window at the hens scratching about in the yard, coffee cup in hand, when the stranger comes and plants himself down in the doorway and offers his wares, wicker baskets, here, have this one it's cheap, the Lord will reward you. A gypsy with coal-black eyes and a whore's smile, hair curling against the back of his neck, wide shoulders, thin hips in the trousers wrinkling over his feet.

Offers his wares.

Opens his pants.

The Lord will reward you.

Brings out the Blessed Sacrament.

Show us the fruit of thy loins.

That the devil and all his works must have extracted from his sleep, he was versifying at a poem that he was doing his utmost to remember, getting up early, scribbling all day, amazed at the sumptuousness of the Word, like a child at a peacock in his pride, I can still see him at his table which he called his desk then at noon heating up the previous day's stew then snoozing before his walk, versifying, hiccuping, versifying, then once again scribbling by the fireside with a blanket over his knees and the wound in his heart that never heals.

Eyes of anthracite, a whore's smile.

He planted himself down in the doorway.

That the devil and all his works.

But prayer, he said, is only a way of landing on the banks of Eros, a whole conventional hodge-podge, the bleating of a frustrated old nanny goat, it moves along unknown paths and ends up in the skin quivering under the partner's caress, the gardener of the enclosure hidden from prying eyes, where a lilac is in blossom, and wallflowers, and daffodils, the scents of aromatic herbs, we shall knock down these enclosing walls so that everyone can enjoy them, he's talking nonsense the neighbors said, how can you expose yourself like that, someone will end up telling the police.

Then the gendarme came and he scratches his head, doesn't know what to say to the gentleman who offers him a drink, sit down, gendarme, what brings you here. The fellow stammers the sergeant sent me but don't go thinking, just gossip that's for sure, the law is the law, that someone says he saw a person walking around with all due respect in the neighborhood dressed in nothing but dark glasses, have you by any chance seen him, the sergeant you know, or the neighbors, they get ideas into their heads, it wouldn't surprise me, you know their daughter's mad, the one that calls herself a poetess, he pronounced it poytess. Miaille gave him a sideways look and laughed up his sleeve or even bursts out laughing, he says they certainly do have bees in their bonnets over at the neighbors' but rules are rules, it's all right it's not your fault.

Or that in fact he might have seen someone at nightfall down by the river, was it a man or a woman, he only had a back view, who did seem not to have much on but with this heat and given the isolation of the place really that wasn't anything to get excited about, in any case as I said night was falling and my eyes are so bad, have another drink.

The white figures.

The rider with the bleeding head.

The poetess pulling up her skirts.

Or the Savior disfigured by torture.

His circumcised sex organ.

But the town was still smoking under its ruins, the old nightmare would reawaken, with the grinding of teeth, this past to be dissolved as it was no longer part of the system, roots plunging into nothingness, the future likewise.

The blackbird whistled Rise.

He rose, went back to the little road that leads nowhere, saying I shall be the strongest, chafing at the bit, restraining his tears, I have always been an exile, we shall make a virtue of it, only absences comfort you.

But someone had seen him in the moonlight.

It was the gypsy of that morning who hadn't found anywhere to sleep, his baskets on his arms, he is whistling between his teeth so as not to frighten him, goodness says the other, still in the district, did you have a good day. The Romany replies no but we're used to it, he was looking for a barn to spend the night in, Miaille indicates his own within a stone's throw, there's some nice fresh hay you'll sleep well there and tomorrow morning a cup of coffee. The man thanks him without servility and he adds you wouldn't have a drop of soup left would you, I haven't had anything to eat today. So it was in company that the sedentary man retraced his steps, they go into the kitchen, they heat up the stew and while he's eating the basket maker tells him about his wife and child, he's left them with some friends not far away, a few kilometers, to make it easier for him to get rid of his baskets here, he's giving himself one more day and then he'll join his family and they'll go south, the horse too needed a rest. But Miaille wasn't listening to him, he was concentrating on something else, perhaps his tone of voice which recalled other similar ones, those destinies you know by heart and which are recounted in the same way, gently, without bitterness, lying words perhaps but what does that matter, they come from the same desert and go back to it in the same way, a former Eden still perceptible but only at long intervals, it has disappeared from people's memories, it only now and then manifests itself in a voice, an inflection, an accent, a second breath, a semi-silence and then nothing, nothing, go back into your wife and into your desert, the Lord will reward you.

That voice under the ruins.

He adds that he had had dealings with the gendarme, the swine said he'd seen me naked in broad daylight, he wanted to take me to the police station, I got your neighbors to intervene, they had to admit that at the time he was talking about I had fallen asleep under the walnut tree in their field within a stone's throw of here and that they had seen me later going off to the hamlet with my baskets, cops are all the same, always setting traps for you but I know them, I don't fall into them any more.

But Miaille wasn't listening to him, he was concentrating on something else, a bizarre image that was taking shape somewhere beyond his interlocutor, it was growing, it reached the top of the walnut tree and then went on up to the clouds which it transgressed, and was now installed in the corner of the firmament where the troop of horsemen was scattering, but it was unclear, troubled, weak, Proteus of despair.

The image, perhaps, of the exiles pursuing their funereal itinerary, an agglomeration of bodies round a common soul, an indistinct cluster, their hopes reduced to that of surviving, from one cemetery to the next, then leaving behind those who can no longer follow and elevating themselves by some malefice of which they are the victims up to the sterile heights, their prayer become absurd, a *ritornello,* a wailing litany whose words are scattered like a string of animal droppings in the infinity of the nightmare.

In the semi-obscurity of a chapel this silhouette on his knees before the Immaculate Virgin, the murmured prayer could be heard echoing other murmurs elsewhere, everywhere, depurative, purgative, lenitive, consoling, somniferous, that of exiles of all kinds, the dispossessed of love, after the exile of this life show us Jesus the blessed fruit of thy loins.

He is there in front of the kneeling man, points to his circumcision and the other plunges, communes with the Sacrament, what is left of all those fine desires, what is left, the town was smoking under its ruins and the orant remained hanging from the Lord's phallus imploring his mercy through the intercession of the queen of angels.

In the semi-obscurity of a chapel the child in front of the miraculous statue, a bunch of poppies in his hand, he stands up and places the flowers on the altar then he lights a candle, his lips could be seen moving, he murmurs his prayer, sighing to the depths of his exile, the horror of the past centuries had become his, a nightmare inculcated by mercies of all kinds, nothing will be left of the eager little heart but a purulent wound, the old obscenity become a cult object, obsessional, celestial and without hope.

Go back to your desert.

Our poytess he said is certainly still religious, you can see her in the church all morning in front of the statue of the Virgin murmuring things to her, she brings her flowers and burns candles, some say she's not quite right in the head but it's nothing to get excited about, whether she spends her time there or anywhere else, I'm not saying she isn't odd with that tic of shutting her eyes whenever she's talking and her stockings rolled down over her shoes, she's rather slovenly but then artists you know.

Now the said lady collected licentious photos through the intercession of you know who, she had a whole album of

them which she used to look through in the evenings while
she was thingummying herself or God knows what it's her
business because when it came to piety no one had anything
on her, she spent all her mornings praying in the church in
front of the crucifix in the aisle, the one on the left as you go
in, some people even claim that she was giving herself an
eyeful on account of the suggestive shape of the cloth you
know where.

And the other evil spirits.

The universe crammed full of malignant powers spying
on us at every turn, that's a very sad view of things, said our
poytess, even though she rolls her stockings down over her
shoes and smells of slovenliness what does it matter, no one
has anything on her when it comes to charity and her poems
which she published as they say in her youth bear witness to
a soul totally dedicated to the Lord, she hasn't changed at all,
a little girl, yes, becoming sweeter all the time and totally
penetrated by her vocation which might well be sainthood,
it seems she eats nothing but the eucharist in the mornings
and three potatoes in the evenings, there's a review or what
do they call it a periodical which now and again still asks her
for a poem to fill a gap so the mischief makers say,
personally I'm sure they print them because of their intrinsic
merit, she certainly saves the odd lost soul who reads her
verse in which the cherubim speak and the Creator smiles at
the least little thing, a forget-me-not, an ant, a speck of dust.

She could be seen at the table in her provincial sitting
room surrounded by old-fashioned odds and ends and
Louis-Philippe furniture, shelves, knick-knacks, dolls won
in raffles, shawls on the pouffe and on the divan, all the
apparatus of the oriental smoker which had belonged to her
late father, doilies, seats covered in *petit point,* potted palms,
sitting at her table and writing to a woman friend or
scribbling notes or churning out an elegy, in her inspiration
she raised her eyes to a black framed engraving above the
chest of drawers, Saint Mary Magdalen repenting in her

grotto, and in the corner of the sitting room the inevitable piano that had belonged to her mother, a gramophone with a horn, scores in the music cabinet and a stuffed cat on a little Moorish style table.

The collection of licentious photos.

Because with old maids of that type say what you like they all have their moments of depravity these moments being bedtime unless they become neurotic it's one thing or the other, which doesn't stop them being pious but I'd be interested to know what sort of images they see behind their eyes when they're praying, even so, whatever I may say....

A little girl becoming sweeter all the time.

Which prowl about in the world to corrupt people's souls.

Went the rounds of the farm buildings again at nightfall, brooding over his nightmare, there were absences in my life which were a comfort then there was a presence that ruined me.

So the voice in the ruins was two.

Then the sedentary man said to the Romany sit down you'll have a drink won't you, the other man told him the story of his life as if it were anyone else's, these destinies that you know by heart, gently, without bitterness, he recognized or wanted to recognize his own life in it, a former Eden lost to memory, all that nauseating hodge-podge which makes you tremble, a wife and child left with friends, he goes off up hill and down dale offering his wares and plants himself down in the doorway, here I am.

So he apparently went to live with this Miaille or whatever his name was, having no ties of any sort, Providence is good at arranging things even though the malady is incurable, and he was the maid and the gardener, every evening from then on was counted as the annunciation of a new life, a face in whose eyes you recognize yourself, the same substance, the same liking for being yourself together skin against skin caressing the night which is softer than the corolla of a lily.

The time is still not ripe.

This present that made him speak, not to know any more what it is composed of.

And he in his turn tells the unknown man the story of his life, a ton of vomited sugar or a stinking defecation. And there they both are, transferred into the days preceding the Fall, and they lived without fear as they had recognized one another, each in his turn following the barbaric horsemen or cultivating the kitchen garden where the aromatic herbs grow or lying in the wood watching the archangels disporting themselves, poppies grew out of their foreheads and cornflowers out of their groins, space had reblossomed, the seasons were solidifed like the salt in which what you have to call happiness is macerating, no other mask.

To follow step by step the exodus of the dispossessed from one cemetery to the next, picnicking on the gravestones, in the same way as you listen to your blood beating on the pillow, sleepless nights, the funeral cortège that will only end…But even though this whole hodge-podge is so fatiguing, to forget it would be to risk sinking the boat, I see it, frail as it is, holding its own on the water but at the mercy of the wind, no compass, its only guiding light the setting sun.

Now the miraculous statue had come down from its pedestal under cover of the night and had slipped out of the church, it had reached the port where some sailors had taken it on board, the queen of mercy, it is sailing now toward those far off lands which are the meeting places of exiles of all kinds and dreamers of nightmares, planted with spindly, sun-parched trees, any corner of cool shade is a miracle there, the Immaculate Virgin would create one for her devotees, listen to their murmur, it's a sort of humming sound in the vale of tears, the plaster cast haloed with stars will soon be found at every crossroads holding out its thousand arms to the weeping faces, *Salve, spes nostria, Salve.*

As he arrived one morning coming from the ruined town he notices some laundry hanging from the windows, the chimney is smoking, the gate into the kitchen garden is open. He goes up and plants himself in the doorway. I, says he, am the owner, then thinking better of it, I have this house, then this house, he starts stammering seeing that the Romany welcoming him is living in it with his wife and child. Do have a drink. Going into the kitchen then where he doesn't recognize any of the furniture, he sits down on the chair they indicate, takes with both hands the glass they offer him. And he listened to the other man doing the honors of the house, we're short of staff, a maid and a gardener if you're interested. Miaille said nothing, listening to the procession of words in that endlessly repeated phrase, not a single one was omitted, so that was what it was to occupy a dwelling-place, a measured formula, concrete and mysterious, it is everywhere, in the bedrooms, in the attics, in the barn, articulated by the slightest draught, inhabiting the silence of the beds and the wardrobes, the sole mistress of the premises. And he tried in vain to repeat it, the words wouldn't come any more, Eden lost from his memory. Then he said I will be the maid and the gardener, my luggage is outside the door, I will have a hole in the hay to sleep in and my knapsack under my head full of café bills and letters to the deceased.

Then the cycle recommenced with the roles reversed, he got up in the morning and ran from the cowshed to the pigsty and from the barn to the stillroom, he didn't stop until evening when his broth was served him under the eaves, the other man refused to be in his company, then he went and slept in the hay where the old obsession materialized, to come back empty-handed to his point of departure, even so he considered himself lucky to be within four walls but how long would the other's whim last, one day with a gesture he would make him clear out and once again take to the road that leads nowhere.

Old obsession.

The cycle in reverse.

So no one would ever speak again of the master and the servant, derision, but of the occupant and the exile.

But he gives a start, he had been talking in his dream and he rubs his eyes while the heavy ship sailed away from the banks with its plaster statue, it would land somewhere else for the glory of Eros, others would mistake it and mumble a shamefaced prayer, show us the fruit.

Dictating the letter in love with itself, that poisoned phrase which smacks of the sentimental picture of Narcissus, he's seen lying on his side, he's admiring himself in the crystalline water in question, a foul pond that ducks dabble in, then he stands up with his latest victory in his eyes and goes and fornicates in the wood or gratifies himself by watching other people fornicate, his pleasure only springs from his own image which he himself has slowly destroyed.

A long time before he went away said the stranger to the new occupant I had known that I wouldn't survive him. And I didn't survive him, it is someone else who is speaking today for the man I was, that's proved by my presence in this house that I no longer recognize, you are in charge of it now.

He opened his knapsack in the middle of the night, the moonlight wasn't bright enough for him to make an inventory of its contents, shone the beam of his torch over his letters and slept no more, sleep forsakes unhappiness.

But he gives a start, he had been weeping in his dream and he rubs his eyes, what was all that about an occupant and an exile and that theory about naked archangels, celestial barbarians, and flowers in inappropriate places, what was that endless lament of a woman or a cow in heat, who dictates these lamentations, what charlatan has undertaken my destruction and is whining these litanies of the dispossessed at me.

For he didn't recognize his own sleep any more, someone else's sleep had smothered it, he is moving about in an enemy dream full of pitfalls.

FABLE

Never spoken that language.

Images that recur like someone else's obsession, what to do with them if not tame them but despite his efforts they retained their barbaric impression. It was then that Narcissus came back to his mind and he leant out over the balcony to look for him on the shore. He was there, at the very edge of the water, lying on his side.

They went to join him and amused themselves by shouting obscenities at him from a distance. The sun was oppressive, the sand burning hot. They went nearer and were suddenly stopped short by one of them crying out, he's dead. And they saw the lifeless pupils and the half-open mouth. His hair was plastered down over the back of his neck, his right hand clenched on his thigh. They gently carried the body up through the sand lilies, holding him under his arms, and put a white cloth over his face. Summer had given way to autumn and mists were rising from the sea, the hills on the horizon had disappeared behind the low clouds. The time of exile had returned and long cortèges were moving throughout the region and converging on the corpse, all finally forming a circle around it as its brothers do around a dead swan.

I can still see them, he said to the unknown man, they're wearing pink or blue headdresses and some of them are draped in long mantles, they're carrying bags made of plaited straw where they put their food. My eyes are riveted on the unclothed men, they are all skin and bone and their genitals are bouncing up and down between their thighs like overripe figs. They are as beautiful as the dead in the Orient. They are coming to bear witness. And the unknown man asked what it was that they had witnessed, but the other had either forgotten or pretended that he had, too many memories were besetting him and he felt as if he was choking.

The past to be dissolved and the future likewise.

When you go up from the sea to the hills you see the full

extent of the dry, white countryside. The cortèges proceed laboriously like caterpillars in the hollows of the valleys. There is something floating in the air which it is difficult to give a name to. Death is everywhere.

The Narcissus in question had become multiplied on the shore which was covered with corpses. The odor spread all over the countryside. It guided the cortèges to the littoral, and the fête would continue for ever and ever.

Et verbum caro factum est.

Its creation, said the Romany, was always imperfect, always needed to be saved, we are inextricably linked to its sin.

The most beautiful of the children of men.

It would eternally start anew with the most beautiful phallus that had ever existed. The tabernacle. He didn't even trouble to do up his buttons, the whole lot was exposed to the sunlight and the people intoned *o salutaris.*

The Romany was watching his host out of the corner of his eye.

This desert to enter naked, dispossessed, without memories.

I saw him he said taking off his clothes which he put on a clump of thorns and start walking but from so far away that I might have mistaken him for his comrade, they were of the same height, the same leanness, the same silhouette. And I imagined that they had both taken off their clothes and were going off in opposite directions to find in the antipodes, far from the dunes and hills, that part of themselves that one represented for the other. But it was an illusion. The lost half was lost forever and their exodus could only end in renunciation.

The hermit had taken up his quarters in the wooded region, so well hidden that what they call a stroke of luck was necessary in order to find him. But *I* say that this stroke of luck is none other than identification, you can only find the hermit by suffering his solitude, the movement is

31

unique, produced by a single mechanism. And that is the illusion.

Miaille listened to these simple words and accepted another drink that the other man poured for him.

The number two, the most imperfect of all.

And the notion of a homeland is dwindling, any sort of identification has become impossible.

Unless the hermit himself cultivates it, warped by his sorrow, and welcomes the exile as his double, everything would have to start anew, go from division to division, and culminate in the mortal number, one plus one equals nothingness.

Or that Narcissus is not dead and is still admiring himself in the stinking pool *ad vitam*. Give him our whole attention. Would thus be the key to the problem, multiplying his forms on the shore, each form preoccupied with itself but giving its neighboring ones the illusion of a crowd, like the cortège of the dispossessed.

He would go the rounds of the farm buildings again at nightfall but without haste from now on, having no more illusions. But perhaps the illusion of someone else would come and put a temporary stop to this quest for nothingness, a fine comedy, from one nothing to the next by way of these insubstantial passageways.

Started to appeal to the phantasmal plaster cast that seemed to be holding out its arms to him, he was raised up into the evening air and flew over the area in which only the chimeras were moving, the kitchen garden, the courtyard, the barn, the little wood, the road that leads nowhere, it comes out on to the desert in which no directions have been marked, you just go around in circles with the sun, the spindly trees have turned into one single tree, you come around to it again with every cycle, and also the dells, that shallow declivity called the vale of tears by exiles of all kinds.

This house would only have existed in a dream in the rutting season, an Eden lost from memory, open to everyone according to his desire or to his pain, but vanished the next day, they thought they still lived in it but it was the house that was eternally dissolving into the shadows.

A formula drained of all sense.

To come back empty-handed.

Flying over the area of chimeras he could have put it all together in the space of a postage stamp, a stamp which to have done with logic is stuck on to the corner of the love letter, the address is only legible to Narcissus, who is decomposing on the bank of the pond.

Then he saw the naked boy opening the letter but not being able to read it, his eyes were closed for ever, he went on breathing for a few seconds and then collapsed, his mouth open.

We pulled him up on the bank, said the Romany, and gently carried him back among the sand lilies.

The white cloth over his face.

The belated traveler must have discovered them at this funereal task, he would have asked no questions, would have withdrawn and continued on his rounds at the far end of the farm buildings, he'd turn left on his next round and from then on would continue his walk into the desert, believing he was still encircling the house, but it had faded away with Narcissus's breath.

A lot of people have been drowned, the Romany went on, and all at this spot, you only have to wait until the storm is over, you never come back empty-handed.

And Miaille compared those hands with his own, which had been carrying corpses for so long, but dream skeletons are so light, you barely feel their weight, you might think your hands were empty even though they're carrying a heap of carrion.

And they're so heavy, the other man continued, you've no idea, you can barely lift them, and as hard as wood, you feel as if you're carrying a great wooden beam.

Or a gallows.

FABLE

That cross planted in the middle of the hills.

The blessèd fruit was nailed to it.

What had he been witnessing.

Something anterior, the other man said good-humoredly, hence never in the past, eternally in the future, a meaningless action which, as it is propagated on the surface, is destined to plunge into the abyss, in other words nowhere, into the interior, everything that it might engender and in the first place the Son of Man, that precarious meaningless sin, the position of witness having been created by this broken-down mechanism before time began and therefore being for ever inaccessible.

Then he hadn't actually been a witness of anything, Miaille uttered timidly.

No replied the Romany, seeing that he was only an accident.

But the other was glancing into the courtyard and said the pigs have broken through the fence, let's go and deal with them.

And Miaille got up, he'd be the swineherd, and he brought the animals back into the enclosure in which there wouldn't be any more aromatic herbs. And he questioned himself about the source of his memories and the angel at his side guffawed, we'll give you something else to think about, Miaille begins to grumble, the angel's voice has become familiar. So it was I says he who was creating chimeras in my own image, I shan't be taken in again.

The next morning as he was extricating himself from his hay and rubbing his eyes he sees the angel fast asleep, he goes up to him, shakes him by the shoulder and shouts I'll give you something to remember too. Now it was the boy with the delphiniums who woke up with a start, Miaille muttered an apology. The boy stood up, grabbed a fork, pretended to threaten him with it and went out of the barn. And Miaille followed him long after he had disappeared.

It must be one thing or the other he said. Either nothing

34

of what I've seen since I came back has any reality and I have only myself to blame, or let's say my state of health, or else everything is happening as if I hadn't come back, is following its normal course, and I am only an imaginary witness, far away from my carcass which is getting on with its own business elsewhere. A choice has to be made. Time for choice. That sort of nonsense. He was dunking his bread in his coffee, sitting on the edge of the wine press, with his washed-out blue eyes, his shoulders hunched up, in his skeleton-like emaciation he looks like....

Two generations of clear conscience and of combat.

That's when the head begins to rot.

In outer darkness.

Rejected by himself, emptied of his breath or of what he took to be such, he could be seen in the mornings limping along on his rounds again, his hair unkempt, his beard pepper-and-salt, and some said that he wasn't really suffering, people questioned him about the trifling incidents of the day, he answered unwearyingly everything's fine. A sneer had got stuck at the corner of his mouth and stayed there even when he was asleep.

And followed him long after he had disappeared.

I never loved you.

Started reading again and got to the point of confusing the narrator's voice with his own, did *I* formulate that rotten cowardly idea, what for, and plunging down into the gulf again and facing the angel he tried to avoid the fatal words that rang in his ears but which according to the destiny of things that have been said could only be resaid, what those fatal words conveyed had to be digested along with the rest.

Took up his pen again, then, and tried to recast the phrase so as to avoid the words that always came back implacably as the basis of the new law, you never loved me, the shadow was our prey, how could we digest the carrion and accept our destiny that resulted from things said.

He must really have been out of his mind then said

FABLE

Miaille, however you look at yesterday, it still remains formulated *ad vitam* and digested as such, the possible interpretations being nothing but a maniac's game, words can't change their places once their bodies have surfaced, what on earth is he looking for, a skin that isn't his own, a mirror in which he'd see himself without any wrinkles, a fairy story for a well-behaved child.

Now the Romany was guffawing and Miaille didn't recognize his face any more, some words *have* changed their places he said, and here is the new skin that might have been mine, we must go on conjuring destiny, it won't have the last word.

To expose Miaille's mistake.

To expose the mistakes of exiles of all kinds, they have never left the places they are weeping for.

A pure maniac's game.

Yesterday and today unformulable, we are contingent.

Nibbling dry bread and weeping endlessly.

The torch, its perpetual comings and goings until dawn over the papers in the sack. Looking for a way out of this labyrinth of utterances. No way out in the direction already taken. Try the other way.

Suddenly he stops seeing everything as consecutive, painfully linked together until its relentless end, and begins to see it as a suspended event, open dwelling-places where he can go from one to the other, he finds himself in each one, his place will not be taken from him by the tribulations to come, the accidental no longer triumphs.

And the other man is there too, as serene as he was the first day, he's been caught in the trap, he is the soul of each dwelling-place. Several identical faces in the mirror of whoever looks at them, unity has been recaptured.

Here the fable could end but it is already trembling from having been stuck on to a moral.

To move words around, a sublime game.

To inhabit every utterance so as to give it its own meaning.

After that he was no longer the plaything but the player, no longer an exile from a problematical country but all the time finding his native land under different skies, buzzing with loved voices which he found pleasure in locating and then in joining, his ear subtly trained. Reencounters and reminiscences.

Where you are, there I shall find myself.

And he was tempted to turn this little victory into a triumph.

The torch would still be moving over the writings in the knapsack, café bills, postcards, hurried rendezvous, all he would read into them now was an endless homily.

Never spoken that language. Something is giving, somewhere.

Or else, considering the battlefield he wondered where he'd come back from and the angel answers from the depths of your carcass, not many come back from there, you have that privilege. And Miaille thought he could have done without it, he was still shaky from his Second Coming.

After the exile of this life.

So it's to be started anew he said since I've come back. No taste for it.

Messing about with the fruit of thy loins.

The whole of Creation was spat out once again.

A certain formulation conditioned by the liver, another by the kidneys, another by somewhere else, each organ in a bad state seeking a remedy in words. Hence the discoveries, the fruit of experience, and so one organ is cured at the expense of its neighbor which in its turn, and so on indefinitely. Miaille thought of deciphering diseases by the analysis in question. And searched his sack, but only pulled out bits and pieces, the difficulty is increasing, in inverse proportion. Great mastery needed to detect diarrhea or coryza in a cry. He was thinking of setting up in the village market-place when someone told him that that discipline was already well-known, find something else. But he wasn't convinced. Gave his consultations *sub rosa.*

What of the invocation to the cross, what of that to the Immaculate Virgin? A strange disease triggered by the first cigarette, vague yearnings, suicidal tendencies or quite simply persistent colic. The liver or the spleen or the heart or the stomach, how can you tell. Discovering by artistic means organs that are both nameless and nomadic, not to say highly individual. Your stoliver, your epiheart, your thyrocardium, your kidnanus.

O crux ave. My pancrenum hurts.

Other utterances would refer to nobler and more furtive organs, the moment you put your finger on them they're already far away. I love you, a specific utterance, would refer to the most volatile.

Centuries of avalanches.

The battlefield.

This phrase, dug out of the fathomless depths of consciousness. Spread out over the surface, a shot-silk effect composed of lymph, sweat and sperm, only ever known under that appearance, a thin film, it reveals nothing of its origins, why make it issue up from the depths, its very being is display, that of the sublime game with which we espouse every utterance.

In his school homework, with its collection of lines, circles, curves, or better still of apostrophes and commas, he would find the ineffable weft, warp, web of concomitant, coexistent, interchangeable states, all his diseases or what people call by that name laid out on the market stall, health being considered from now on to be like a game of hopscotch or tapestry.

Divine spider.

It jumped from one thread to the next, finding a fly, its sustenance, caught in each one. But you still had to think of it. Your chronology is so anachronistic, said the spider, I control space.

The spider's only enemy is the broom, but it loses no time in secreting an identical surface elsewhere.

He saw the condemned couple silhouetted against the sea, each had his arm around the other's shoulder and was absorbing through his eyes the mortal element in which they hoped to find I don't know what viaticum. Indefatigable enemy, the sea ruins everything it penetrates.

Maris stella.

Azure death.

The exiles also ploughed through the waves which were becoming stained with the blood of the dead, chopped up by the billows they had been returned to the sand on the shore, no contamination tolerated by the liquid element, putrescence would be returned to the earth.

The stunted tree standing erect in the middle of the ocean can be found in every cycle. It bore shell-fish and worms for fishermen. They supplied themselves from its branches. It disappeared during the night under the eyes of the exiles who heard it groaning until morning. It was the tree of life.

Or the gallows.

To sink like a stone as you approach it with no ulterior motives, that demands the humility of the beggar. A worm, spare a worm for your humble suppliant. O God, our refuge and our strength.

And the Savior would dispense his worms as soon as someone pronounced the formula in the right way.

True, fishermen, he knows all about them, said Miaille. Gallows birds. Vermin of every description.

Such cowardly remarks by way of prolegomena, on the wrong track.

Miaille was to be found, after the flight of the gypsy, reknotting one by one the threads of the cobweb, relearning the formula, this dwelling-place that is our own, but now only occupying the attic. By an unexpected sublimation, the house's foundations were apparently no longer in the ground in the courtyard, but one floor above, aerial, floating, the garret having become the ground floor. And people going for walks under the house would look up and believe they were seeing a rain cloud, or a fog, or some other such vernacular phenomenon, it would be written up in the local newspaper but our poetess would be the only one to penetrate the enigma, being quite familiar with levitation etc. Hiccuping, scribbling, bleating, slobbering, never leaving her Louis-Philippe sitting room, she must have become the instrument of a tyrannical muse, she was no more than skin and bone, yet her poem would no longer be an obscure idyll but become rock-hard.

We saw the sibyl in her socks, we asked her what sort of weather it would be tomorrow.

We saw the sibyl in her mittens, we asked her what God's secret name was.

We saw the sibyl in her woollies, we asked her what to do with our carcasses.

She answers unwearyingly that the present time must likewise be dissolved, put on your sandals and gird up your loins.

Meanwhile Miaille was spinning his web. One morning he grows spiders' legs and his abdomen is full of eggs, so now he's the father of a whole tribe. He has his own place by the fireside, where he sits in state rather than shivers with cold, and dispenses justice to his people. Couldn't you please tell me, grandfather, how to solve my problem. He replies unwearyingly nothing equals zero, tracing a great big circle in the air in front of him.

The poetess visits him, they both laughed like idiots. That ridiculous secret they shared.

Compact and without fissure *in aeternum*.

The couple formed by Miaille and the sibyl.

Corpses cast up on to the shore. Formula of the

massacre. Every morning at the feet of the Immaculate Virgin invoke the Evil One. Barter the old man's soul against these ivory and ultramarine bodies. The statue with the plaster eyes won't be able to see beyond the end of her nose, led by the troop of the dispossessed she'll go off to the antipodes to bless the sea there. As for the licentious photos, put them as an ex-voto under the pillow of the subject, who will get into bad habits. Comfort of the afflicted.

Vessel of honor. A clandestine octopus had taken up its quarters therein. Nourished itself on the corpses' sperm. And in fact when they were cast up on to the beach their balls were missing. People made guarded allusions to it. Such as wondering what connection there might be between the octopus and the Immaculate Nomad. You can very well imagine the two of them arguing over who should have the lion's share. But all the plaster arms can grasp is just wind. The others are suppler. Is it still the Romany speaking, Miaille wondered, I thought he'd gone. But voices last much longer than carcasses.

Then Miaille, nauseated by the wiles of the octopus, disgusted with the passions and weary of the so-called sublime game, went to consult the hermit in his retreat. He adopts a serious expression, dusts down his clothes and knocks on the door. He waits for a time. Then out of the adjoining little garden comes an individual that gives him the cold shivers, it has several arms, its head is somewhere between its thighs, it drags itself along with the help of crutches or oars, as if creating around itself the element in which it has its being. Every movement it makes is accompanied by a groan and it comes and coils up in the doorway. Are you the occupant asks Miaille. I am whatever you want me to be replies the other, don't you know that, after all those years furrowed in your face. Don't be the octopus says Miaille, I'm tired of its wiles, be compassionate.

Now the door was open and by the fireside an old man was meditating, sitting hunched up on a stool. Neither your wrinkles nor your arthritis impress me said Miaille, I can show you just as much of both if you like, wisdom has no mask, be compassionate.

Now a young man who moved like a girl was arranging a bunch of flowers in a vase. Miaille hesitates before saying anything, he observes him. Then an unexpected feeling of repulsion impelled him to say that's enough of this nonsense, Narcissus no longer fills my sleepless nights, be compassionate. The other looks at him and starts laughing, his garment falls to the ground, his body is seen to be covered with pustules. Miaille thinks for a moment and repeats: wisdom is nothing to be ashamed of, I'm tired of deformities, my own are quite enough of a burden.

He knocks on the door. It opens and someone he doesn't see asks him to come in, a hand takes hold of his and leads him to a chair on which Miaille sits, he's waiting for the light to be turned on to his host's face. But the host says what are you waiting for, your eyes closed when you knocked on my door, you will never see me, speak if you accept me as being as blind as you. And without a moment's thought Miaille said I'll stay, my luggage is by the door, go and fetch it and tell me which corner of your room I can make my own, peace has returned to my spirit.

This house which is ours. This voice which is mine, this skin which I caress and which does not flinch. Mirrors have become useless, and subtleties of language, and the fear of being hurtful. The one and only response is formulated from dawn to dusk by the one and only host, they have merged into one other.

Until the day when the desire to see is no longer taboo, that desire is acute. The door opens and Miaille is thrown out.

Then of his own accord, without a moment's thought, he puts his own eyes out with his knife.

Looking for somewhere to spend the night he stopped by a wall, ran his hand over it, found a door, went in, made a hole in the hay and fell asleep in it, his knapsack under his head.

But someone had heard him, a belated traveler perhaps.

The town had evaporated as a result of a cataclysm, nothing was left but the dross, it was rough to the touch.

They said that little groups of people were camping in the ruins. The man called Miaille or Miette[2] went off with his stick looking for a convenient path which would enable him to join them, he explains that he has nowhere to sleep any more, he would be satisfied with a place amongst them. The response is immediate, stay here you can be our bard. This impromptu baptism looses the blind man's tongue and he starts singing. They lavish attentions on him, they caress him, they put honey in his milk. For so long as he makes them dream of their lost homeland he makes them forget the very notion of it. But then they begin to find his recitation monotonous, you don't want the same images over and over again for ever, they ask him to change his tune, he forces his talent, which has become mannered, they stop caressing him and the day comes when they serve him his milk without honey, and then water it, and then cut it out altogether. He whines for his pittance like a dog, he sits up and begs, he does a jig to make them laugh but these tricks soon lose their effect, he stays in his corner by himself, he waits for death. It comes, and carries him off. This is when a boy, poking about in the knapsack, finds his notes which they decipher, the poems are restored to their original form, the people celebrate the memory of the bard, his tomb is bedecked with everlasting flowers.

This future to be dissolved.

Did he think about it before he fell asleep or did he only rely on the few rhymes at his disposal to conjure his public.

He sees again that bleeding head being carried off by the naked horsemen, he recognizes it as his own, one stroke of the knife was enough to open his eyes, those that are not dazzled by the sun.

FABLE

And the phallus eaten by the chief was also his.

I am that new kind of Narcissus he said, deprived of his eyes and of his favorite organ, the fable is tempting. And there he is, thrown into that starless world in which his forms are dispersed, he will go feeling his way toward his arms and his legs, trying to reunite them with the beloved body and then to give the corpse back its breath. All his wanderings will be nocturnal and no matter which way he turns he will always land on the shore where from amongst the lifeless corpses he will choose this head of hair, that ear, that phalanx, which he will graft on to his carcass and then feel himself dissolve, his quest will have become vain.

To know why the cataclysm in the town.

Asking the exiles is useless, they speak another language.

Threadbare old string of an instrument eviscerated by the barbarians.

To patch up the sound-post, the soul of that viol or fiddle and to produce harmonics from the newly-tuned string. Piecemeal suggestions of the original melody, a path to venture down so as to recognize the old haunts, palaces, alley-ways, gardens, market-places. He sets off.

On his right once he had passed the crossroads there would be a working men's district built of blocks of concrete. Particular resonances, brief echoes, trenchant voices not a single word of which is lost. To transcribe these everyday remarks. Housewives, craftsmen, commercial travelers. Threadbare conversations.

On his left there would be a square. Trees in blossoms, public benches, lawns. Lovers, nursemaids, children. Same language. Onomatopoeias. Threadbare.

Further on on his right one end of a bridge over the river. A barrel organ, a blind man turning its handle. Groups of students. April light. Threadbare.

Further on on his left an office building. Midday. Time

44

for the gentlemen's aperitifs. Naive, sentimental atmosphere. Threadbare.

Further on on his right the old clock tower. Tourists waiting for a series of ridiculous carved wooden figures to come out of the box. Celebrating the culminating point of the day. Comments and historical references. Threadbare.

Further on on his left the station with its tumultuous evocations. Holiday time. Either coming back. Or going away again. Or coming back again. Ditto.

Further on on his right a café terrace. Sounds of mouths, forks and knives. Snatches of conversation between two slurps of soup or vanilla custard. Joy of living-eating. Ditto.

Further on on his left. Ditto.

Further on on his right. Ditto.

The town has been resuscitated. Cataclysm unexplained.

I'm listening, he said, I'm listening, a muffled lament isn't enough, I need audible words. But no one is going to say poppies and cornflowers any more, I shall have to hold out my hands and feel their slender corollas, the dreaded laceration will be inscribed in the stones along the path, everything is against me.

And he lent an ear, it had been affected by centuries of avalanches, the only things that surfaced now were high-pitched whistles, squeaks, sawing sounds.

Threadbare.

A blackbird whistled three notes.

Early morning walks come back again, picking mushrooms, coffee in the corner bistro, a few laughs fade away in the forest.

A blackbird whistled three notes.

Resolutions made; dignity, a touch of genuine stoicism, the morals of an old monkey, rotten to the core, the only things that surface are the convulsive movements and hiccups of the moribund. Old crackpot.

A blackbird whistled three notes.

FABLE

This chronometry to be dissolved.

To rediscover in the depths of the lost years Narcissus's grimaces, he communed with the sand lilies and other purities that shall remain nameless, resolutions of an old monkey, hiccups of a chronometer.

I want said he a new fable. It can only arise out of the ruins.

Compact and without fissure *in aeternum.*

How would our old poetess have put it asks the schoolboy. He is sitting hunched up on his chair by the fireside, frozen with cold under his crocheted shawl. Let things find their lowest level. That hodge-podge that has got so long in the tooth when he. When he. His ear is becoming more acute.

Nothing. No way out.

Eyes no longer dazzled by the sun.

The exiles are running through my head, he said, that draughty cavern, that closed-in space through which the cortège passes at staggering speed, unless they are permanent picnickers leaving piles of greasy papers and orange peel while they keep harping on about their lost homeland, what a farce, and are as static as boundary stones, their faces pale with anemic fat, the inspired ones prophesying and the rest getting more and more sluggish amongst the smells of muck and ham, the exodus has become nothing but a threadbare old story, that's what I've been reduced to.

Now our poetess was rushing about all over the place, we'd meet her at the crossroads, old nanny goat with her beard and her droppings, her chaplet of rhymes between her gums and her dentures, she mumbles at staggering speed, pulls her diary out of her reticule, scribbles, hiccups, splutters, and splashes about in her petty little poem, the completely imaginary misfortune that at the time of unsatisfactory loves she attributed to heaven with all its pomps and works, a lyrical, erotic and shitty hodge-podge in which her solitary, distorted soul went zigzagging.

46

Between gums and dentures.

She meets the fellow called Miette at the crossroads, that old crackpot with his beard and his tics. He's as blind as a beetle since the business with the knife, she doesn't realize it at first because he's wearing glasses. Says something to him about his reluctance to greet her. You used to be more polite. He makes a vague gesture in front of him which is quite clear, she falls over herself in excuses. He asks her to help him over the crossroads, a reminder of the town in this deserted place. Our poetess with one hand grabs hold of his arm and with the other wipes away a furtive but compassionate tear. Weep for your sins says Miette abruptly. He had adopted a Biblical tone, the old duffer with his funny fur hat. The rhymeress no longer has the slighest doubt but that he's lost his marbles and she muttered have pity on him.

Our refuge and our strength.

Threadbare.

She meets Miette at the crossroads. This was before the Fall. Between gums and dentures he mumbles some word of abuse when he sees her then greets her ceremoniously. She goes on her way, absorbed in her poetic knitting. He no longer has the slightest doubt but that she's lost her marbles and muttered have pity on her. When suddenly there he is, blind. And what follows. These sorts of reversals that throw light on things in depth. Nonsense.

She meets him at the crossroads, still before the Fall, and both being deep in their own meditation thinking they'd only seen the other in spirit continue on their way and imagine what follows, abuse or civility, until the moment when in fact either looking back or on the way back, supposing that one of them hasn't moved any more than a boundary stone, he sees her, she sees him, both are privately amazed at the coincidence, the marvels of the unconscious, that psychological and shitty hodge-podge which so many solitary, distorted natures delight in.

She meets him at the crossroads. He doesn't move any

more than a boundary stone, either waiting to cross the road or absorbed in a painful meditation, the caprices of fortune, the night that is leading him to death, the fate that was his even before he had opened his eyes, that tough, specious hodge-podge in which he would flounder even when able-bodied and in the prime of life. In short, she goes up to him and says something civil. He starts, and lets off the fart he had been incubating, hence a brief show of bad temper and on her part either a scandalized reaction or a discreet withdrawal or both but only so very slightly discordant that an observer wouldn't have known what to make of it, maybe thinking she was deaf. In short, she goes off and imagines how embarrassed she would have been if she had been in the blind man's place, forgets her original assumptions and starts wondering about this or that while Miette who has been disturbed in his favorite occupation goes on cursing the tactless woman. Unless, forced out of the sluggishness which his sedentary nature delights in, he reacts unpre-dictably and for some reason which has yet to be explained accepts responsibility for the tough, specious assumptions of our poetess and reproaches himself for not being what a well-intentioned third party might imagine at first sight, as for instance an old blind graybeard who transforms his melancholy into philosophical and resigned thoughts, so as to achieve resolution, dignity, genuine stoicism, to develop in that sort of direction from now on, at the same time giving up bothering about unsatisfactory health, and all its pomps and works.

Between gums and dentures.

She meets Miette at the crossroads. For some reason that has yet to be explained she imagines herself in the person of the old graybeard with the twitching eyelids, she becomes a prey to a terrible anguish, a warning if that's what it was that she had had that morning when she couldn't read a headline in the paper, blindness is staring me in the face, I'll be like that any minute now, for the impulses that direct our compassion toward other people come from our own *amour propre* and return to it. She goes up to the blind person, hiccuping and slobbering, and mutters a distressed word that the person addressed takes to be his own at this precise moment. Concordance between his meditation and the compassionate phrase. So I was talking out loud he says, which is what our poetess in her turn is convinced that she has said, and there's a fine subject for those who have a taste for erotico-hallucinatory grimaces.

Of Narcissus tempted by the Bible.

Would find there something to satisfy his passion by the roundabout way of the chimeras. A kind of pleasure in condemning himself and then immediately absolving himself in a flood of tears. Fits of repetance full of promise. Fits of false candor allied to collusive phantasms.

The figure lying by the edge of the water is insistent. Today it is leaning over the Book in the guise of a mirror. Discovers in it that his eyes are more penetrating, his nose more delicate, his mouth more thick-lipped. Words in the guise of the silvering of a mirror, words which reflect his splendid image while his carcass is disintegrating and his flesh dangling. He doesn't yet know the power of the Word which restores his illusory youth and incites him to complacency.

Heretical theme. Something is giving, somewhere.

The lies of the Word. He finds himself in many phrases. Is going to be resuscitated by a miracle. Nonsense.

Leans over the Book, then, his ear subtly trained, and leafs through the pages he is listening to, reminiscences, to trace the portrait of his opaque face. Is rewarded with a doubly factitious view. Then he gropes about in the sand, finds his stick, stands up and goes back to the hut which serves as his shelter. He will fall asleep in the company of this phantasmal double, the corners of his mouth turned up in a sneer.

Narcissus become old.

FABLE

The images of the night.

What of the observer in the moonlight.

He too had aged, he didn't move any more than a boundary stone, at his post for a long time, taking root in the putrescence of the trunk he was leaning against, an old watchman of nothingness, his old head in which the conformists of the drama are shaking with fear, a meticulous orchestration, absurd, with no echo.

Where are the sources of information in all this hodge-podge he said, blindness is not my strong point, but that's what it will have to become.

Miette searched in his sack, passed a finger over all the papers and infallibly pulled out the letter. Worded like a popular almanac. Some charlatan must have dictated it. Spell out every word. Between gums and dentures. Trembling mandibles, sputterings, whistling noises. Chaplet of droppings that precedes his sleep then sprinkles it with chaotic appoggiaturas. He is heard spluttering, groaning, puffing and blowing. The letter has been put back in its place but the finger on the blanket is still following the transcribed treachery, line after line. When he wakes up the graybeard opens his knapsack again, takes out the letter and keeps harping on his degradation the way people keep on scratching themselves. He gets up and goes out into the courtyard where the echo of this litany, amplified by the night and by all the dead years comes surging up from all sides. Groping, he makes his way from the wine press to the stables, from the stables to the hen house, from the hen house to the barn. The hole in the hay. He stoops, his hands recognize the place, he tries to muster up his memories. He farts and laughs. Stands up again and calls out to the Romany, we'll give you something to think about. The Romany said he needed someone to help him. His wife and child. What has become of them said Miette, I must have dreamed that story of the occupant, never left the place I weep for.

Narcissus petrified on the edge of the pond. Exile isn't his strong point either. He's covered in droppings. Birds come and perch on his head and peck at his ears. A duck has been hatching her eggs between his legs and her ducklings are playing with his phallus. A couple of meters away the observer sitting on a camp stool is tracing the portrait of the forsaken man. His eye-sockets are blank, his face gnawed by vermin.

This chronometry to be dissolved.

The images of the night.

Monsieur Miette said the child, I saw him he came back one morning on the seven o'clock train, Baptiste and I were washing Monsieur Chinze's dog and then all of a sudden he was tapping us on the back with his stick, where is Louis from the bar he said, take me to him at once, personally I'd never seen him but Baptiste remembered his voice from when he was a kid, even so it was a bit odd, the old fellow with the beard who can't see but who knows everyone, he told us that's Latirail's house and that's old Lorpailleur's garden, that's the baker's and that's the laundry, he could almost have gone round on his own but as he said in your days there are too many cars, take my hand.

Because *his* days, Baptiste said, were the old days, before the cars and the holiday makers, before the hotels and the campers and noise everywhere, my father told me and that's what he's always said, he must remember Fantoine before the beginning of the world, and *his* time has got stuck somewhere.

And when we got to Louis' he kissed him and that was a bit odd too, the two old boys in each other's arms, Louis was crying but not Monsieur Miette, he straightaway said give me a coffee what's the use of getting sentimental we'll talk about all that later, for the moment I've got to think about finding somewhere to stay, Louis said yes yes all right, he told us that in the old days Monsieur Miette was quite someone and everyone used to say how d'you do to him,

51

nowadays he's the only one who knows him it's the revenge of this one and that one it's the revenge of.

It's the revenge of our modern times, said Baptiste, when the old families that used to work for Monsieur Miette and the craftsmen and the cheap stores have got rich, they don't need him any more, my father says that good manners have gone out of fashion, old men like Miette, we don't have to suck up to them any more.

But Louis, the child went on, said that if you don't say how d'you do to Monsieur Miette and if you don't give him a hand when he moves in you can say goodbye to cokes in the bar and I'll give you something to think about, because he hadn't got rich and Monsieur Miette was his pal from when it was their days.

So we took Monsier Miette to his house Louis still had the key and the old man ran his hand over the walls the place smelt of mildew and there were mice and spiders' webs but he was pleased, he said make a fire in the hearth and warm this up for me, it was a mess tin with a lid that he'd taken out of his sack there were some beans in it I think my sister came to make his bed she said the sheets were still in the cupboard all right all except the pillow cases she couldn't find any my mother lent him one of hers.

And now Baptiste added he never leaves his house he knows all its corners by heart we aren't allowed to disturb him, for the difficult things he asks Louis who sends Loulou or he goes and has a drink with Monsier Miette himself, they sit for hours in the kitchen garden telling each other their stories, as my father says it's the last stage before the, it's the last stage before the.

It's the last stage the child said before the last.

His pal from when it was their days.

Because it seemed that he had actually built his house with Louis who knew about such things, there was a carpenter in those times and a mason and a lot of people who are dead or have gone to live in the town, our village has been taken over by the holiday makers who buy everything from the supermarket where it's very expensive, I mean the little things, for the real work you go to the big firms in the town that charge you for their journeys and for their phoney sundry expenses and even for their so-called studies in schools or God knows what, whereas before you were just a local craftsman with no frills, they used the local stone and the wood from the forest, these days they say it isn't any good and it seems that stone is too expensive, it's still the same though and there's so much of it that no one knows what to do with it but there you are, they belong to their own times and the strangers who build houses, what would they know about the Rouget quarries, they never go over that way, they don't go for walks, they go to the bars in the town, as proud as anything when they say we're going to our country place, but their country, they've made it completely artificial what with their swimming pools and their patios and solariums and I don't know what, it hasn't a single thing in common with the real country.

It was a poor part of the country where you weren't very warm in winter, where you stayed indoors in summer, where on Sundays you went on excursions to the forest or the mountains, you had your soup when you came home and chatted about the various events, the Bianle girl's marriage, Magnin's new horse, old mother Migeotte's accident, it wasn't exciting as they say but at least you knew what people were talking about, whereas these days they argue about politics in the Middle East or American negros while they're eating their Cape lobsters to the accompaniment of their transistors, they haven't the slightest idea about anything, they don't know the names of the trees along the wayside, or of the little morning and evening breeze, they don't know what the berries or even the trout and the partridges of the region taste like, they buy their grub in the town and the more it's like everyone else's grub, the more it's processed or deep-frozen or God knows what, the more easily they digest it so it would seem.

He knows all its corners by heart.

Obviously after all that time and even though he'd been away from it for years it comes back to him through his fingers and through his head, he runs his hands over the walls, he counts the steps, the house as it was in his days comes back to him with a lot of things that no one can see, it's full of people and murmurs and sighs, so many lives insinuating themselves into it or hiding or blossoming like delicate flowers, a curtain startles them, a draught makes them move aside, a tick-tock awakens them and starts them roaming noiselessly through bedrooms and corridors, they sit down in an armchair for a second, they caress the piano, they leaf through an album and pff, there they are shoved back into the closets, Monsieur Miette has migraine, he walks up and down, he ruminates, he makes himself a cup of herb tea, he sits down again by the fireside, he calms down, the dance starts up again, it develops, he's no longer alone.

This joy that was mine.

Voices behind Sinture's house, I can recognize Poulot's, and Louis's, and Mahu's, any minute now they'll be in the bar on their way back from the railroad where they work. Wind in the corner of Monsieur Songe's wall, it makes the dead vine and the satin flower shrub vibrate. A smell of garlic and fried food. A slight draught under Mademoiselle Miaille's door, she covers her shoulders with a shawl. The moon has risen, three fellows are still in the bar talking about hunting, everywhere else the lights have gone out. This is the time when the old men are sighing, when the young ones are going off to the town, when the mountain seems to settle down on its foundations, its foothills reach as far as the Rouget valley and Grance. The forest awakens its witches and the far-off sea is setting inoffensive waves in motion. People have forgotten the midday bells.

He sits down again by the fireside, he calms down.

This voice that was yours.

My life has been over for a long time, you sowed a seed of the future in it but it didn't take.

Flowers on the walls, branches, fledglings. The silence outside augurs nothing, now. The stones are slowly dying, they're either splitting or rusting, no doubt about it, their metamorphoses don't bother us any more, one fine day we say well well, it isn't the same any more.

When Baptiste came back the next day to sweep the courtyard Monsieur Miette called out something to him, the young man went up to him, the old man was still sitting by the hearth, his fire had gone out, he hadn't eaten his beans. Light it again he said, you don't know how to light a fire any more, and go and fetch me some bread from Philippard's, I don't want anyone else's. Now Baptiste didn't know anything about Philippard, the only baker he knows is Doucette, he went and saw Louis who said ask for a well-baked loaf that's what he likes, he won't know the difference, don't bother about Philippard it's ages since he gave up his baker's shop and he's dead like the rest of them. And Baptiste went back with his loaf and Miette ate a mouthful and said no one knows how to make bread like Philippard, you must take me to see him later on, I'd like to shake his hand.

And Baptiste said later not being much good at expressing himself but being sensitive for his age that he had had a vision of Monsieur Miette going the rounds of the cemetery and shaking the mitts of all the dead people surrounding us in a vague place between heaven and the tomb where he himself would be tomorrow, holding out his hand in his turn to the last survivor so that this old prehistoric story, this story of Fantoine before cars and water and electricity and all the din shouldn't be immediately forgotten but brought back to mind up to the very last by the people who had loved it and, who knows who knows, miraculously saved and transmitted by one of us, maybe even the most stupid, but not the most heartless.

He added that Monsieur Miette wanted to make some changes in his hovel, that'll cost him something but he's never been really hard up, that old fellow won't take us in any more. Unless he's getting gaga. To have work done on your house when you're on your own and with one foot in the grave. Seems he still has some nephews but he never sees them, quarreled with his family. Is supposed to have said he wanted to talk to the mason and the carpenter. Louis had no alternative but to tell him that neither one of them was still alive. But the old man gets stubborn, he'll go to the nearby hamlet where you can still find craftsmen.

And in fact one morning Baptiste saw a couple of men from Malatraîne talking to the old man under the lean-to, we know now that he's going to have a salon built if you please, with three windows plus a french window opening on to the courtyard plus a manor house fireplace that the mason demolished at Mademoiselle de Bonne Mesure's, because of the new taxes she's getting them to pull down a more or less ruined hunting lodge in her forest.

Thus Monsieur Miette who we thought had come to the end of the road, blind and crippled, is taking on a new lease of life and spreading himself, which could be a lesson to a lot of people but which isn't because all the old men around our parts are poor.

A black salon said our poetess to the sewing-circle ladies, the reason being that as he can't see anything any more, that would be appropriate don't you think, with the motto embroidered on the cushions and screens, Nothing can touch me further, and nothing further can touch me, like that royal widow you remember in the history of France[3], our poetess could be venomous when she felt like it and her audience laughed but none of them knew the famous motto, culture not being the strong point of the ladies round our parts which in one way we may deplore, polishing the furniture and doing the cooking is all very well but spending all day on such activities hardly elevates the mind and a few high ideals wouldn't hurt anyone, I'm thinking of their husbands who as *they* have no chance of any leisure would thus find in their wives, instead of money-grubbing, scandal-mongering old shrews, wise women who would temper their passion for lucre and redirect to some extent their thoughts from the sordid worries which in spite of everything these unhappy men carry with them all their lives, thus finding themselves at the end of their days more lacking in intelligence and liberty than pigs being led to the salting tub.

Yes she continued that old duffer when you think how he's been sneering at us all his life and now just look at his latest invention, what's he going to do with his salon, keep his tom cat in it I suppose, all that sort of thing ought to be taxed, the State isn't doing its job, it ought to be teaching these plewtocrats what stuff our common people are made of because don't you realize, it's the electors that count and three-quarters of them are for the opposition, our old common sense isn't dead, the day will come when equality will triumph, long live the Internationale. And the ladies trembled, our poetess was laying it on a bit thick, in any case what had Miette's extravagances got to do with the end of the world, because for them that was what the triumph of justice meant, the hordes coming surging up from you know where, burning down the villages and violating the convent school girls, the result of their divagations as newly-enfranchised voters, you discuss things in the sewing-circle, you go in for politics but the words which are several centuries out of date for the people who only use them when the occasion arises, between a braised beef and a trip to the grocer's, lead you in that domain as in plenty of others on to the apocalyptic spectacle of unbridled passions, odd isn't it, anyone might think that the moment you give people something to think about that has nothing to do with their daily routine, all they can come out with *ad vitam* is such idiotic remarks

conveniently dug up from the ancient depths of private
horrors.

When Baptiste came back the next day to sweep the
courtyard he went straight to Monsieur Miette who was
turning over in his mind the idea of the salon by the fireside,
he said just like that, animated by the love of the truth you
owe to the people you respect, and ever since the business of
the cokes Monsieur Miette was sacred to him, my mother
says that our poetess says that the electors say that
plewtocrats. Don't be an idiot said Miette, just think and
come out with it, what plewtocrats, what electors, what is all
this farrago. But Baptiste didn't know any more. Then
Miette said, I'll tell you what she trots out, our rhymesteress,
she says I'm an old crackpot or duffer, that I'm having a salon
built in my house which won't be any good to anyone, that
it's a crying shame, that the government ought to do
something about it, and do you know why, because she
hasn't got a sou, because she's pretentious, because her
poems as she calls them are rubbish and don't sell, and
because what she calls her mind, far from being full of
beautiful things, only delights in other people's misfortunes
under the pretext of humane feelings. And Baptiste was
convinced.

When Baptiste came back the next day to sweep the
courtyard Monsieur Miette called out something to him, the
young man went over to him and the old man said these
plewtocrats, we'll teach them what stuff our common people
are made of, the electors are for the opposition, the hordes
will come surging up to violate justice, long live the
Internationale.

You understand he said to the child, people repeat what
they've been told, they just don't have the time to go and see
for themselves, listen to me, or they don't take the time, so
they call me Miette like someone or other took it into his
head to do one day, they don't look any further, now my
name is Narcissus, I'm telling you this under the seven seals

of secrecy, are you capable of holding your tongue, I'm not the person they think me, a simple case of substitution, I'll explain one day, that's where we've got to. And Baptiste was convinced.

This chronology to be dissolved.

When Baptiste came back the next day he went straight to the barn, he opened the door, he saw a man asleep in the hay, he didn't dare wake him up, a tramp or a gypsy, he quickly shut the door again and he waited outside until it was time for Monsieur Miette to get up. When the old man's shutters opened he ran up to the house, he said there's someone sleeping in the barn, I don't know who it is, shall I turn him out. He saw the blind man's face become strange, his eyebrows rising above his blank eyes as if he were waking up a second time, his mouth opening as if he was going to speak but nothing came out, Baptiste was frightened, he waited for an answer, first of all Miette shook his head and then he said very slowly so it is he, so it is he, everything is starting all over again. And he stayed at the window with his eyes wide open on what they saw within. Baptiste began to sweep the courtyard.

Later the old man opened the kitchen door and called out something, Baptiste went over to him, the blind man said lead me to the barn. And Baptiste took him by the hand and led him there, he opened the door but the tramp had gone. Where is he asked Miette, he must be there, and he walked to the right, stooping, but Baptiste said he must have run away when he heard you call out, he was in that hole yes in front of you, you've found the right place. Because I know it well said Miette, leave me I'll call you. And Baptiste went off to finish his sweeping.

There in the hay only waiting for the night.

No one to turn me out or to keep me here. The terrible story is repeating itself, everything is starting all over again.

A tramp or a gypsy as they say without looking any further. Narcissus came here to die.

FABLE

His face gnawed by vermin, his eye-sockets blank. The carcass is leaning on its side, the movement it makes to look at its reflection in the water. There are screech owls' droppings on its skull.

Centuries of avalanches.

Put a white cloth over his face.

Monsieur Miette called Baptiste back, you must keep a closer watch on the barn he said, we'll put a padlock on it, I don't want any tramps here they might set the place on fire. And on his way back to the house taking the child's arm he was muttering things the boy didn't understand.

And in fact one morning Baptiste saw two men from Malatraîne talking to the old man under the lean-to, Miette was explaining his ideas about the salon, they'd rescue some beams as well as the fireplace from the hunting lodge in the forest, it was pure profit for the proprietress. Narcissus Thiéroux the carpenter later said to one of us that if the old man wasn't losing his marbles at least he had some pretty strange bees in his bonnet, after the discussion about the building materials he asked them into his kitchen for a drink and enlarged on the idea he had at the back of his mind, a salon he said with mirrors on all sides, something I imagine like all those mirrors they have in fairgrounds the carpenter commented where you see your nut from all angles, comic idea for a blind man, but he'll have to pay, there's no doubt about that, he immediately suggested the first third in advance, the second when the work was half-completed and the last on delivery.

Thus Monsieur Miette who we thought had come to the end of the road.

He gets up in the morning and goes and runs his hand over the walls of the lean-to so as to be penetrated by all that stone, all that mortar, all that wood, the better to buttress his dream, he calls Baptiste, asks him to measure up here and there, raises his head and staring at the rafters with his dead eyes he imagines the ceilings of the great houses in the olden days, he stretches out his arms from one window to the next, he counts his paces as he walks up and down the mud floor, we must have the most beautiful tiles there, there oak panels, there a skirting-board, there a cornice, and for the furniture, he said to the child, we'll go round the antique shops, there are at least a hundred in the district, I'll teach you the trade. And Baptiste in his mind's eye saw a cathedral being built, he mentioned it that evening to his mother, adding one of those remarks that was sensitive for his age that Monsieur Miette when he was talking away like that, raising his arms and staggering all over the place, made him think of a bird whose wings had been clipped, people would built him a cage that was much too big, an aviary where the cripple would stay crouching down by his little water bowl and where all the space would be occupied by spiders.

You understand said the old man people repeat what they've been told, a misfortune for instance, they say it's a testing time or just something you have to put up with as best you can, they don't look any further, but misfortune has no date, it doesn't arrive one particular day and fly away another day, it's there, it doesn't budge, we experience it or not according to unknown laws.

And Baptiste was convinced.

Notes

1. page 2   "This Miaille or whatever his name is"...The author seems to have no particular verbal harmonics in mind when giving Monsieur Miaille his name. But he likes the association that occurred to the translator: Miaille—Maille. *(Une maille* is a stitch, a thread).... "Divine spider. It jumped from one thread to the next" (P. 25) "Meanwhile Miaille was spinning his web"....(P. 26)

2. page 29   "The man called Miaille or *Miette* went off with his stick." *Miette:* crumb, shred, tatter, remnant.

3. page 39   "Rien ne m'est plus, plus ne m'est rien." The motto adopted by Valentine Visconti, Duchess of Orleans, after the murder of her husband on the orders of the Duke of Burgundy, Jean Sans Peur, in 1407. The Duchess was the mother of the poet Charles d'Orleans, and she died of a broken heart the year after her husband's murder.

The author now disapproves of the sometimes blasphemous tone of this book.